Halloween

story and pictures by Miriam Nerlove

ALBERT WHITMAN & COMPANY, NILES, ILLINOIS

For Hannah, with love,
and special thanks to Ann

Text and Illustrations © 1989 by Miriam Nerlove.
Published in 1989 by Albert Whitman & Company,
5747 West Howard Street, Niles, Illinois 60648.
Published simultaneously in Canada
by General Publishing, Limited, Toronto.
Printed in the United States of America.
10 9 8 7 6 5 4 3 2 1

Library of Congress Cataloging-in-Publication Data
Nerlove, Miriam.
Halloween! / written and illustrated by Miriam Nerlove.
          p.   cm.
Summary: In this rhyming story, a little girl and her parents
experience the excitement of Halloween night.
ISBN 0-8075-3131-6 (lib bdg.)
[1. Halloween—Fiction.   2. Stories in rhyme.]   I. Title.
PZ8.3.N365Hal   1989   88-36858
   [E]—dc19   CIP
                                                    AC

HALLOWEEN! HALLOWEEN!
Let's get ready for Halloween!

Pick a pumpkin from the patch—
the biggest, roundest of the batch.

Then carve on it a funny face

and put it in a special place.

Now let's decide—what shall we wear?
A witch and monster make a fine pair!

You wear this monster mask—
it's green and big.

I'll wear a rubber nose
and a long, black wig.

See Daddy putting on your mask?

Oh, no...

Daddy's gone! Where did he go?

There he is!

The stars are out, the moon is high.
It's time for us to go outside.

Ghosts and witches, fairies and monsters...

We've all come out to trick or treat,
to fill our bags with lots to eat.

Let's walk next door and ring the bell.
"Hello, Mrs. Green! Trick or treat!" we yell.
She gives us fruit and something sweet,

then we knock on doors

all down the street.

It's darker now and getting late.
Let's go back home where Daddy waits.

Look who's glowing with a grin—
our pumpkin's glad we're coming in.

And Daddy, too!

Let's dump our bags onto the floor.
Your bag's not empty—see, there's more!

Now take the green mask off your head.
It's time *this* monster got to bed!